DINO RIDERS

How to Catch a Dino Thief

Don't miss:

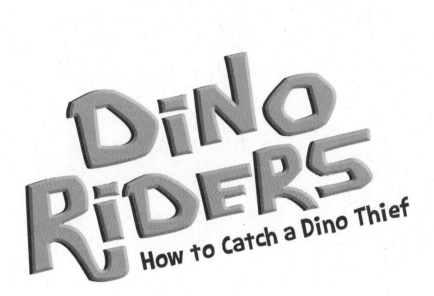

How to Catch a Dino Thief

Will Dare

sourcebooks
jabberwocky

Published by Sourcebooks Jabberwocky, an imprint of Sourcebooks, Inc.
P.O. Box 4410, Naperville, Illinois 60567-4410
(630) 961-3900
Fax: (630) 961-2168
www.sourcebooks.com

Library of Congress Cataloging-in-Publication Data

Names: Dare, Will, author.
Title: How to catch a dino thief / Will Dare.
Description: Naperville, IL : Sourcebooks Jabberwocky, [2017] | Series: Dino
    riders ; [4] | Summary: Josh is determined to capture the Blood Claw
    Bandit and use the reward money to help fix his family's ranch, especially
    after Josh's beloved triceratops, Charge, is stolen.
Identifiers: LCCN 2016030791 | (13 : alk. paper)
Subjects: | CYAC: Dinosaurs--Fiction. | Robbers and outlaws--Fiction.
Classification: LCC PZ7.1.D32 Hk 2017 | DDC [E]--dc23 LC record available at
https://lccn.loc.gov/2016030791

Printed and bound in the United States of America.
VP 10 9 8 7 6 5 4 3 2 1

With special thanks to Barry Hutchison.

The Lost Plains

here be dinosaurs

N
W · E
S

Scaly Point ◉ Settlement

more Wandering Mountains

Wandering Mountains

Roaring Jaws Valley

Cold Fear Forest

Scratchclaw Swamps

Trihorn Settlement

Trihorn Road

Sanders' Ranch

Iguanodon Plains

Loneheart Lakes

CHAPTER 1

Josh Sanders crouched left in the saddle, steering his triceratops, Charge, around a jagged rocky outcrop. Charge's enormous feet thundered across the dusty ground as he hurtled through the twists and turns of the Roaring Jaws Valley.

"Yah!" Josh shouted over the booming of Charge's footsteps and the roaring of the T. rexes on either side. "Go, Charge, go!"

Josh spun in the saddle and looked back. Right behind him, his all-time hero, Terrordactyl Bill, raced along on his own fully grown triceratops. T-Bill gave Josh an encouraging nod, then flicked the reins of his dinosaur. He and Josh dodged and weaved side by side through the maze of rocks and boulders as the snapping jaws of the T. rex army drew closer!

"Giddyap!" Josh snapped his lasso at the closest tyrannosaurus, and the brute jumped back in fright.

"Good idea, partner!" cheered T-Bill, unhooking his own rope from his belt and cracking the air in front of another of the beasts. The tyrannosaur turned, spinning its long tail around like a whip.

Josh looked up ahead to where the landscape widened out into an open plain. They were nearly through the dangerous valley, but something was blocking the way. The whole end of the valley was lost in a cloud of…

Uh-oh.

As the wind whistled around him, Josh realized what he and T-Bill were running straight into. "Tornado!" he yelled, but it was too late! A swirling cloud of sand was lifted up into the air, choking him, blinding him, and scratching at his skin.

Josh turned, holding up his arms to protect himself. "T-Bill?" he cried, but his voice was swallowed by the storm. "Where are you?"

The whistling sound rose to a scream. Josh

peered up through the sand cloud and could just make out a tall tower spinning toward him. The wind hit Josh with the force of a charging triceratops. It wrenched him from the saddle and—

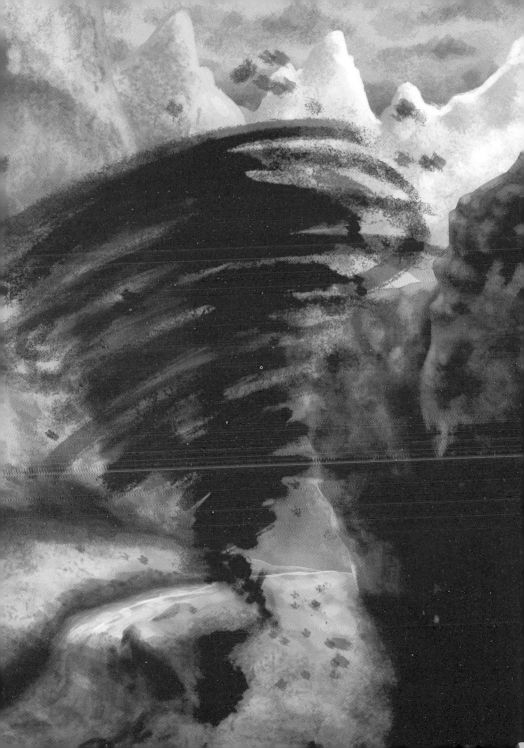

Josh jumped awake with a yelp.

"Yargh!" he cried, still half-asleep. He was breathing heavily, and his back was wet with sweat. He glanced around his room and let out a sigh of relief.

"Just a nightmare," he whispered. Then he frowned. If it was just a nightmare, then how come he could still hear the wind?

Josh leaped out of bed and ran to the window. Through the grimy glass, he could see a towering tornado, just like the one in his dreams, only this one was tearing across the family's field. The swirling wind ripped up rocks and plants as it carved its way across the grazing land.

"Oh jeez!" Josh cried. "A twister!"

He didn't have time for outdoor clothes, so he raced outside in his pajamas without a second thought. The wind howled around him so strongly, he could barely move his legs to walk. The dino pens lay halfway between Josh and the twister. The iguanodon herd would be panicking, Josh knew. If they stampeded, the whole herd could get lost across the Lost Plains. He had to act fast.

As he ran, Josh could just make out Charge thrashing and tossing his horned head around in his pen. Josh couldn't help but smile. The brave triceratops was actually trying to fight the storm!

Ducking his head, Josh ran for the pens.

He pumped his arms and drove forward with his legs, but he still felt like he was running in slow motion. He listened for the bleating of the guanos, but all he could hear was Charge's snorting and the whistling of the wind.

Reaching the barn, he tucked himself in behind it, using the shelter to catch his breath. Charge's pen was just a final short sprint away now, and he could hear the dino snarling and snapping angrily at the raging storm.

There was another sound too—the *bang, bang, bang* of hammering from somewhere close by.

"Josh! What in the name of the Lost Plains are you doing out here?" called Dad.

Josh looked around then up to find his dad

gripping the roof of the barn. His mom's head appeared over the edge too.

"What are you doing up there?" Josh shouted.

"Making sure the roof stays put," Mom explained. "If we lose that, we can kiss every-thing inside good-bye."

Josh understood. The barn was full of the crops they'd gathered at the last harvest. They couldn't afford to lose that. The barn was also where they kept the food for Charge and...

Josh suddenly realized why he couldn't hear the iguanodon herd. His eyes widened, and his mouth hung open.

"What is it?" asked Dad. "What's wrong?"

"The guanos are still out there," Josh said, pointing toward the field where the beasts were grazing. "They're right in the twister's path!"

Mom and Dad exchanged a look of horror. "Aw, no," Dad cried. "Then we've lost 'em for sure."

"Not yet we haven't!" Josh said, rolling up the sleeves of his pajamas. "I'll get them!"

"Josh, no, wait!" cried Mom, but Josh was already battling his way through the wind toward Charge's pen. The triceratops snorted with excitement and rushed out when Josh dragged open the heavy gate.

Charge wasn't saddled up, but there was no time for that. Josh used the dino's horns and armored frill to pull himself up onto his broad back.

"Yah!" Josh yelled, using his knees to spur

Charge into a lumbering run. The tornado seemed to stretch all the way up to the sky, and Josh was close enough now to see whole trees spinning around inside the column of wind. The closer they got, the more violent the wind became, and Josh had never been more grateful for the tough frill behind Charge's head. He ducked low behind it, blocking the worst of the gales.

Up ahead, he could just make out a few guanos cowering together in the corner of the field. Yanking on Charge's frill, he steered the triceratops toward them. Charge bucked his head and bleated, and Josh had to shout at the top of his voice to make himself heard.

"Easy, buddy. You can do this!"

11

The twister was tearing past them up the field now. Josh realized that if they led the guanos back toward the barn, they'd be leading them right back into danger. There was another field over to the east. If he drove the herd out that way, then chances were they'd be safe from—

Suddenly, there was a deafening crack from somewhere behind him. Josh tugged on Charge's fringe, and the dinosaur turned sharply. Josh felt his heart leap into his throat. "Oh no," he groaned.

Josh's mom and dad were racing toward the house, both looking back over their shoulders as the swirling tornado smashed into the barn. The whole structure shook, then collapsed like a house of cards.

A moment later, Josh ducked behind Charge's frill again as the air was filled with broken planks, rusted nails, and the family's entire harvest of crops.

Josh kept low until the worst of the noise had passed. Slowly, he raised his head and peered over Charge's armor. The tornado was veering off to the left, well away from the house. That was the good news.

The bad news was that the barn, and every-thing in it, was gone.

Josh's mom and dad picked through the wreckage of the barn, turning over broken pieces of wood and nails, trying to figure out if anything could be salvaged.

Josh stood to one side with his best friends, Sam and Abi. News traveled fast in Trihorn settlement, and they'd heard all about what had happened to the ranch. They'd come to see what they could do to help fix the barn but had quickly realized that there was no more barn to fix.

"It's fine though," Josh said hopefully. "We can just build a new one. Right, Dad?"

Dad glanced Josh's way and tried to smile. "Uh, maybe," he said.

"Winter's coming up fast," Sam pointed out. "If you don't get the barn rebuilt, the guanos will end up as dino Popsicles."

Abi shot Sam a look. "No kidding, Sam."

They kicked through the rubble in silence until a voice from back near the house interrupted.

"Well, howdy, y'all!"

Everyone turned to see a flame-haired woman in a flowing red coat striding toward them, waving enthusiastically.

 16

"Hello," said Mom warily. "Can we help you?"

"Ain't about how you can help me, ma'am. It's about how I can help you!" said the woman. She grinned from ear to ear. "Or your dinos, at least."

She thrust a hand out for Mom and Dad to shake. "Name's Melissa H. Barnstable III. I'm Barnstable, but—and I hope you don't mind me saying—that barn of yours don't look stable in the slightest. Twister hit?"

"Uh, yeah," said Dad. He frowned. "Who are you?"

"You sent a microraptor message asking for a veterinarian," said Melissa. She bowed theatrically, which made Josh and his friends laugh. "You got one."

Mom and Dad looked the woman up and down. Josh thought she looked more like a circus performer than a vet, but there was something about her he couldn't help but like.

"You're lucky, Mr. Sanders—can I call you Mr. Sanders?" Melissa asked, but she didn't wait for an answer. "Truth is, I travel around lots, and I'm only in town for a few more days. I'm due to head out over the Wandering Mountains before long. After all, you gotta keep those dinos healthy, don't cha, Mrs. Sanders?"

Caught off guard, Mom blinked in surprise. "Um…"

"Exactly," said Melissa. She clapped her hands together, then spun toward Josh. "Now, young man, why don't you and these fine friends of yours take me to the patients while your mom here whips up one of them famous pies I keep hearing about in town?"

Josh looked at his parents. They both shrugged. "Right you are, ma'am," said Josh. He gestured down in the direction of the field. "Step this way."

Along with Sam and Abi, Josh followed Melissa around as she checked over the iguanodon herd. She pulled open the dinos' mouths, peered into their ears, and pried open their eyes. "Yep, all looking good," she said, then she reached into her coat pocket and pulled out a glove. She slipped her hand inside, then unrolled the glove until it covered most of her arm.

"You might want to look the other way for this part," she said, lifting a guano's tail. Josh and his friends turned around, then winced as they heard a squelching sound. The iguanodon let out a yelp of surprise.

"Yep, fit and healthy, inside and out," Melissa declared. She was about to move on to the next patient when she spotted Charge.

He was tethered to a stake where his pen had been and was pawing miserably at the debris of his fence.

"Hello, who's this?" Melissa asked.

"That's Charge," said Josh. "But I wouldn't worry about him. He's indestructible!"

Melissa took off the glove, rolled it into a ball, and tossed it to Sam. He instinctively caught it, then remembered where it had been and tossed it to Abi, who leaped back in disgust.

"I've been all over the Lost Plains, right from one end to the other," Melissa said. "And I've yet to meet anything that's truly indestructible. Mind if I check?"

Josh shook his head. "No. Check away. But trust me, he's fine."

Melissa whistled through her teeth. "He ain't fine," she said. "Look."

Standing on his tiptoes, Josh could just make out a tear between two of the spines of Charge's armored frill. "Looks like he took a hit in that storm," Melissa said, and Josh felt his stomach flip.

"He's gonna be OK though. Right?"

Melissa smiled, showing the whitest teeth Josh had ever seen. "Sure he is. Don't worry We'll take care of him."

She patted Charge on the side, and he let out a friendly snort. "He is one mighty fine triceratops."

Josh's chest swelled with pride. "That he is. He and I won the Founders' Day race together a little while back. He even took on a giganotosaurus—and won! He's the fastest, strongest triceratops in the county. Maybe the whole world."

Melissa gave Charge another pat. "Why, he must be the most valuable thing on this whole ranch, now that the barn ain't no more."

"Yeah, I'd say so," said Josh.

"Now look here." Melissa thrust a piece of paper into Josh's hands. "That's the ingredients for an ointment that I like to call Melissa's Magic Mixture."

Josh peered at the list and began to read. "Garlic, fish guts, iguanodon snot…"

"Gather it up, mix it together, apply liberally," Melissa said.

Josh blinked. "To what?"

"To the wound, of course!" Melissa laughed, pointing to Charge's fringe. "My magic mixture will clear that up in no time." She winked. "That's the Barnstable guarantee." She thrust a hand out, and Josh shook it. "Good luck, Master Sanders," she beamed. "Now I'd best go grab me a slice of your mom's pie, then get going. Pleasure to meet you."

"You too," said Josh.

Abi and Sam came over to join him, and they watched the vet skip back toward the house.

"She was interesting," said Sam.

"By 'interesting,' do you mean 'really weird'?" asked Abi.

Josh smiled. "I liked her," he said, then he

looked down at his list. "Can you guys watch Charge for a minute while I go and see if we have any of this stuff in the house?"

"No problem," said Abi, then she laughed as she slapped Melissa's glove down on top of Sam's head.

Josh headed for the house just in time to see Melissa trotting off on her dinosaur. She was tucking into a big slab of pie. From the smell, Josh could tell it was the fish and veggie deluxe Mom had made the night before. Hopefully, there'd be some of the fish guts left over for the ointment.

He was just passing the kitchen window on the way to the front door when he heard his parents talking. From the tone of Dad's voice, he knew immediately that something was wrong. Holding his breath, Josh tucked himself in beneath the window and listened.

"We can find the money somehow," Mom said.

Josh heard his dad give a long sigh.

"I wish you were right," said Dad. "But the fact is, we've got nothing saved. A new barn's going to cost more than we can raise."

"So what are you saying?" asked Mom, and Josh felt his heart beat three times faster as he waited for his dad to answer.

"I'm saying," said Dad, "that we have to sell the ranch!"

Other Dino Remedies

DR. JOHNSON'S OLD TIMEY ELIXIR

Is your dinosaur deaf as a post? Does he slow down when you yell "giddy up" into his ear? Well, Dr. Johnson's Old-Timey Elixir is what you need to clear that dino earwax outta there! Just one drop and a good scrub will clear out those stinky earlobes for good!

Plodder

Frog Extract Wart Tincture

There's nothing worse than a wart—trust us, we know. But here at Malady and Placebo we have just the thing. Try our brand-new tincture and banish those warts for good. Our unique ingredient of minced frog will get to work in no time. And the broken snail shells will add a nice exfoliating finish.

WILKIN'S MIRACLE RE-GROW

Baldness? Pfft! That's ancient history. In fact, it's prehistory—now that Wilkins's Miracle Re-Grow is here for you. Just add one dollop to a bucket of dino dung and apply liberally to the affected area. Before you know it you'll be hairier than a T. rex on a Tuesday.

gross...

CHAPTER 3

Josh plodded along on Charge's back, heading for school. Sam and Abi trotted beside him on their smaller dinos, doing their best to cheer him up.

"...and then the whole thing exploded in Sam's face, covering him in eggs and flour from head to toe!" Abi laughed.

Sam blushed. "It wasn't my fault. How was I to know it was going to blow up?"

"It was hilarious!" said Abi. She shot Josh a glance.

He nodded back to her. "Yeah," he sighed. "Sounds great."

It had been two days since the storm, and Josh had spent both days worrying about having to sell the ranch. His parents hadn't mentioned it though, and whenever he tried to steer the conversation toward fixing up a new barn, they quickly changed the subject.

"Hey, it's not that bad," said Abi. "I'm sure they won't have to sell."

"Even if they do, what's the worst that can happen?" asked Sam. "So you have to move out of your home, find somewhere new to live…probably miles away in another town, and..." His voice trailed off when he realized Abi and Josh were both glaring at him. "Uh, yes," said Sam, clearing his throat. "Actually, when I put it like that, it does sound quite bad."

"But it won't come to that," Abi promised. "Even if they did try to sell, my dad says there's no one buying right now."

Josh raised his head. He hadn't thought of that. "Yeah, that's a good point," he said, brightening a little.

"Anyway, there's something even bigger to worry about," said Sam.

Josh winced. "Oh great. What?"

Sam glanced left and right, making sure the coast was clear. "You know my dad's the town

clerk, right? Well, he heard that the Blood Claw
Bandit is on the loose."

"The who-called-whatsit?" asked Abi.

"The Blood Claw Bandit!"

Josh frowned. "Who's that?"

Thwack! The wind slapped a large sheet of
paper over Josh's face. Fumbling, he pulled it
away and found himself staring into a drawing

of two dark, mean-
looking eyes.

"The Blood Claw
Bandit," Josh read.

"Wow," said Abi.
"Talk about good
timing!"

Josh continued reading. "Wanted for robbery, burglary, larceny, hold-up, impersonating a kitten..."

"Impersonating a kitten?" Abi spluttered.

Josh read the line again. "Yep. That's what it says."

The others leaned over in their saddles and studied the poster. There was a big drawing of the Blood Claw Bandit's face so people would recognize him. The only problem was, the picture had him wearing a hat that was pulled down low and a neckerchief pulled up over his nose. Only his eyes could be seen, and they were so deep in shadow, they were nearly as hidden as the rest of him.

"I'd heard the bandit was mysterious and

rarely seen," said Sam. "But that's ridiculous. He might as well be a turnip with a hat on for all that picture tells us."

"Is he dangerous?" Josh asked.

"He's as mean as a box of rattlesnakes and crooked as a dog's hind leg," said Sam. "They say a posse went after him out east a few months back, and he left them all tied to a giant cactus. Face-first."

Abi winced. "Ouch."

Before they could study the poster any more, the wind whipped it out of Josh's hands again. They watched it sail off on the breeze, then all three of them shrugged.

"Oh well," said Josh, flicking Charge's reins. "Guess we should get school over with."

BOLO Alert —
Famous Lost Plains Criminals

Tricksy McGraw

Notorious card shark and gambler. No con is too low for this mean and vicious shyster. Reward: $75. Last seen tricking a titanosaurus out of its breakfast.

Harriet "Hoodoo" Hawkins

A no-good hoodlum known for bank robbery and grand larceny. She uses her hypnotic hallucinations to bamboozle bank clerks and control dangerous dinos.

Gang of Gore

They're the Lost Plains' most vicious gang. Holed up in the Wandering Mountains, they ambush unsuspecting travelers and steal everything they've got. And, if they're feeling especially mean, they'll feed you to the nearest T.rex.

The teacher and most of Josh's classmates had heard about what had happened with the tornado. They all shot him friendly smiles when he strolled into the classroom.

At the back of the class though, Josh's archenemy, Amos Wilks, leaned back in his seat and smirked. "Well, well, well," he said and laughed. "Look what the wind blew in."

"Ignore him," said Abi. She and Sam took their seats on either side of Josh as the teacher, Miss Delaney, called the register.

When she had finished reading out the list of names, Amos stuck up his hand. "You forgot Gale."

Miss Delaney frowned. "Who?"

"Gale," said Amos, barely hiding a snigger. "You know Gale, right? He's really tall. Hey, Josh. What about you? Seen any big Gales lately?"

Josh felt his fist clench. "Real funny, Amos," he muttered.

"Yeah, I was up all night barnstorming it," he said. "Wait, I mean *brainstorming* it. I always get those two mixed up."

"That's enough, Amos," Miss Delaney warned him.

"Sorry, ma'am," said Amos. "I wasn't trying to get Josh *all twisted up*, I swear…"

As the morning went on, Amos didn't miss an opportunity to make a dumb joke about the barn getting destroyed. By break time, Josh was ready to wipe the smile right off the bigger boy's face.

"What's your problem, Amos?" Josh demanded as they filed out of the classroom into the midmorning sun.

"Don't try to stand up to me, runt," said Amos, sneering down. "I could blow you over just like that barn of yours." Amos cracked his knuckles. "But in answer to your question, I ain't got a problem. I've got a solution."

Josh blinked in surprise. Abi and Sam, noticing the two boys were facing off, raced to Josh's side. Arthur, who was partly Amos's friend but mostly his loyal minion, scurried over to stand by his master.

"A solution? What kind of solution?" Josh asked.

Amos grinned. "You know my uncle, Malachi, right? 'Money-Maker' Wilks."

"Money-*grabber* Wilks, more like," Sam muttered under his breath.

"Yeah, I know him. He's that slimy, no-good, con man who likes to rip honest folks off, right?" Josh knew Malachi as a spindly, wasp-tongued millionaire from the days of the Great Lost Plains Gold Rush. Back then, he'd tricked people into traversing the dino-infested valleys to get the gold, while he made all the profit.

"That's him," said Arthur, then he shrunk back when Amos glared at him.

"He's a businessman, that's all," Amos said. "And he's in the market to do some shopping."

Josh felt his pulse quicken. "What kind of shopping?"

"Ranch shopping," said Amos, and his eyes gleamed with glee. "And he thinks yours is just the place he's looking for!"

We need to talk," said Mom as she plonked a piece of pickled pumpkin pie down on Josh's plate. It was an unusual pie to serve for breakfast, but Mom's mind had been elsewhere since the storm.

"We can't afford to fix the barn and have to sell the ranch," said Josh, all in one big gasp. He let out a big breath. "I know all about it…"

Mom and Dad exchanged a glance. "Well, we

were going to say that you really need to take better care of your room, but…" Mom sighed. "I guess you overheard."

Josh nodded and pushed his pie around on his plate. "I did," he said. "But it's fine. We can raise the money."

Dad chewed on a rubbery piece of pickled pumpkin. "You got an idea? I'm all ears."

Josh's mind raced. "We could…start a dino circus," he suggested. "There could be an iguanodon trapeze, or I could shoot myself out of a cannon?"

"Hmm," Dad said and smiled. "Anything that doesn't involve you flying through the air with your backside on fire?"

Josh racked his brain, trying to come up with

a solution. He hated the idea of them selling the ranch, but he hated the idea of Malachi Wilks buying it even more.

"A dino petting zoo," Josh suggested. "We could even get a T. rex. Everyone wants to pet one of those, right?"

"Cute idea," Mom said, smiling. "But I think a T. rex might bite your hand off if you tried to pet it."

"How much do we need?" Josh asked, cramming a forkful of pie into his mouth.

Dad cleared his throat. "All in? About five hundred dollars."

Josh coughed as he choked on the lump of pie. "How much?" he asked. Five hundred dollars was more money than he'd ever seen

in his life. He'd have to do more than create a petting zoo to make that much!

A sudden squawking from out on the porch made everyone jump. Bumble, the family's scatterbrained microraptor messenger, flapped in for a landing on his perch, missed, and slammed into the door.

Josh jumped up. He hurried outside and unwrapped the note from around the dazed birdlike dinosaur's foot.

"Anything important?" asked Dad.

"It's from Sam," said Josh, reading the note. "He wants me to meet him in town. Says it's urgent."

"What about chores?" Dad called, but Mom shushed him and appeared in the doorway behind Josh. She handed him his hat.

"If it's urgent, you go for it," Mom said. "And leave the ideas to us!"

Soon after, Charge rumbled along the Trihorn settlement's main street with Josh bouncing around on his back. It was just like any other Saturday in Trihorn. Piano music tinkled out of the saloon, folks moseyed in and out of the general store, and half a dozen dinosaurs drank from the trough set up outside the clerk's office.

Josh swung down out of Charge's saddle and led him by the reins to a tethering post beside the trough. He fed the triceratops a handful of sugarcane, then patted him on his side.

"Back soon, buddy," he said, then he ducked into the alley beside the clerk's office, pushed aside the broken fence board, and slipped into the backyard.

Sam smiled and waved as Josh squeezed through the gap in the fence. "That was quick," Sam said.

"You said it was urgent," said Josh.

"It is," said Sam, nodding gravely. "I was talking to my dad earlier, and it seems someone came into his office looking to draw up some deeds."

Josh frowned. "Huh?"

"Property deeds," said Sam. "To your ranch."

Josh's face went pale. "Who?" he asked.

Sam gulped. "Malachi Wilks!"

Josh groaned. For once, it looked like Amos had been telling the truth. Malachi Wilks—the uncle of Josh's archenemy—was going to buy his family's ranch right out from under them. Josh wondered if things could get any worse when he and Sam heard a commotion from out in the street.

"Stop, thief!" a voice roared.

Josh shot Sam a wide-eyed glance. "A robbery!" he said with a gasp. "Let's go!"

"Let's not!" Sam said, but Josh was already shoving aside the board and pushing his way through the fence.

The boys skidded out onto the street just as a gunshot rang out. Charge and the other tethered dinosaurs snorted and kicked out in surprise. Josh ducked behind a barrel, while Sam ran in circles, flapping his arms.

"They're shooting!" Sam yelled. "They're shooting!"

"Get down!" Josh barked, grabbing his friend by his shirt and pulling him into cover.

A figure wearing a black hat and coat raced out of the bank, carrying a big sack over his shoulder. He had a neckerchief pulled all the way up over his nose and a shiny six-shooter held in one hand.

"It's a bank robbery! A real-life bank robbery!" said Sam.

"This is the most exciting thing I've ever seen," said Josh. It was about to get more exciting too. As the robber ran for his dinosaur—a

muzzled velociraptor that was tied up nearby—
the town sheriff came rushing along on the
back of his gallimimus.

"Freeze, ya no-good thieving varmint!" the
sheriff yelled, but the robber didn't even slow.
He leaped into the saddle of his velociraptor
and yanked on the muzzle.

The raptor spun on the spot and opened its jaws wide, letting out an angry hiss. Startled, the sheriff's dinosaur skidded to a stop. The robber raised his hat in the air and spurred his raptor on. The sheriff gave chase, but the raptor was already pulling ahead. The sheriff's dino eventually stumbled to a stop, while the robber became just a cloud of dust on the horizon.

Josh dashed into the bank just as the teller popped her head up from behind the counter.

"Is he gone?" she asked.

"He's gone," said Josh. "Are you OK?"

The teller stood and brushed herself down. "I'm just fine," she said, "though the same can't be said for Gus."

"Who's Gus?" Josh asked as Sam joined him.

The teller pointed to the wall above them. A saggy-looking stuffed T. rex head was mounted on the wall. In the middle of its nose was a perfectly round hole. It made the dino look like it had three nostrils.

"Poor Gus," the teller said with a sigh. "He's never going to be the same."

"It's an improvement," muttered Josh. Something down on the floor had caught his eye. He bent down and picked it up. "What's this?" he wondered, turning the object over in his hand.

"It's a claw," said Sam. They spotted a smear of blood across Josh's fingers.

"A bloody claw," said Josh.

The boys gasped as they realized what they were holding. It was a calling card.

The calling card of the Blood Claw Bandit!

CHAPTER 5

Josh bounded along the path and jumped the two steps leading up to his house. The piece of paper he held in his hands might just be the answer to all his family's prayers, and he wanted to show his parents straight away.

"Mom! Dad!" Josh called as he raced through into the kitchen. He stopped suddenly when he saw a tall, skinny man in an expensive-looking suit sitting at the head of the table where his dad usually sat.

"Hey, Josh," said a sickly sweet voice from the corner. Josh felt his teeth grind together when he saw Amos sitting up on the kitchen counter. Josh was never allowed to sit on the counter, so to see Amos doing it made his blood boil. "So good to see you, *pal*."

"Josh, this is Malachi Wilks," said Dad.

Malachi peered down his long, crooked nose at Josh, like he was examining something on the sole of his shoe.

"I know who he is," Josh said. "What's he doing in our house?"

"Oh, isn't he a charmer?" said Malachi, the word hissing through his thin lips.

"Mr. Wilks has some good news, Josh," said Dad, but from the way he said it, Josh knew it wasn't going to be good news at all. "He wants to buy the ranch."

Josh's jaw dropped. "And that's good *how*?"

"Because," said Mom, shooting Malachi a smile, "he's going to let us stay here and run the place."

"So you'll be work-ing for him," said

Amos. Josh couldn't miss the delight in his voice.

"For a modest monthly fee," added Malachi.

Josh stared at his parents in disbelief. "So let me get this straight. He wants *you* to pay *him* for the pleasure of working for him?"

"No," said Mom.

"Not really," said Dad.

"That about sums it up," cackled Amos.

Dad tensed and only just managed to stop himself from saying something. He forced a smile. "Josh, why don't you and Amos go play outside for a while?"

"Pah. Not a chance," said Malachi. "I won't have my nephew mixing with this *hooligan*. I hesitate even to have them in the same room."

"Now you wait a minute," Dad said with a growl, but Josh stopped him.

"It's OK, Dad," Josh said. "There's a bad smell in here anyway. I'll be in my room."

Before anyone could stop him, he stomped out of the kitchen and hurried to his bedroom. His heart was racing, and his blood felt like it was on fire. He'd never been so angry. Malachi and Amos were both laughing at his family, and there wasn't a thing they could do about it.

Josh suddenly remembered the paper in his hand. It was all scrunched up in his clenched fist now, but he did his best to smooth it out as he took off his hat and threw himself down on his bed.

The dark eyes of the Blood Claw Bandit glared

up at him from the page. It was exactly the same poster as the one that had hit him in the face earlier, but now the sheriff had scrawled a handwritten comment at the bottom. It was this part that Josh was interested in.

"Reward," he whispered. "Five hundred dollars for the capture of the Blood Claw Bandit."

Josh stared into the picture's eyes for a long time. The bandit was dangerous, that was for sure, but if it meant they didn't have to sell the ranch to Malachi Wilks, then it was worth the risk.

Chances are the bandit would move on to somewhere else soon, so there was no time to lose. Working quickly, Josh scribbled a note and marked Sam's name on the front. He could still hear Malachi talking to his parents down-stairs and knew he couldn't go that way, so Josh crossed to the window and quietly pulled it open.

"Psst. Bumble!" he whispered.

Down on the porch, the microraptor raised its head and looked around, quizzically.

"Up here!" Josh said.

The little winged dinosaur turned its head almost all the way around, searching for the source of the sound.

Josh sighed. Bumble wasn't the smartest microraptor in the county. Truth was, he was barely the smartest microraptor on the ranch and only qualified on account of being the only one.

 63

With a flick of his wrist, Josh scattered some sugarcane down on Bumble's head. The microraptor squawked in surprise, then looked up. Josh beckoned him upward, and after a few moments of unsteady fluttering, Bumble landed on the windowsill.

"Take this to the post office," he instructed, attaching the note to Bumble's leg. "And try not to get lost this time."

Bumble croaked.

"Good boy," said Josh, scratching the little dino on the top of its head.

Josh sat by the window, watching the microraptor fly off in the direction of Trihorn settlement. He knew what he needed to do, and he had a plan about just how to do it. Now all he had to do was put it into practice. And that, he knew, would be the risky part.

Malicious Malachi's Business History

Lil' Driller Diamond Co.

Back in the day, Malachi Wilks made his name and his fortune in the great Lost Plains gold rush. He didn't do any of the hard work, but he did make all the money! Now they search for diamonds in the depths of the Cold Fear Forest, destroying precious dino habitat.

5x Liquor Co. XXXXX

Strongest booze in the whole of Trihorn County.
   Puts hairs on chests.
      And that's just the dinosaurs.

Iron Girders Building Concern

The crookedest construction company in the West. Some call 'em twister chasers. No sooner has a whirlwind brought a building down, then they'll charge you double for putting it back up!

CHAPTER
6

Howdy doodly, ranchers? Anyone home?"

Josh opened one bleary eye and stared up at his ceiling.

"Wakey wakey, Master Sanders! Rise and shine!"

Swinging his legs out of bed, Josh yawned and stretched, then clambered into his clothes. It was so early that even Mom and Dad weren't up yet. He could hear Dad snoring as he darted down the stairs and out into the yard. The sun was just peeping over the horizon, and the ranch was still mostly in shadow.

Melissa Barnstable, the vet, waved at him from down in Charge's pen, her red hair shining even in the dark. When Josh joined her, he could tell she was worried.

"There you are. Didn't wake you up, did I?"

"No," said Josh. "I've been up for hours."

Melissa smiled. "Is that a fact? Well, good for you, Master Sanders."

Charge trotted over and lowered his head so Josh could give him a pat. "Morning, buddy," Josh said, fighting back a yawn. He looked over at the vet. "Is everything OK?"

Melissa made a weighing motion with her

hands. "Yes and no. Did you use the ointment like I said?"

"Every day," said Josh. "Mom helped me mix it."

Melissa brightened. "Teamwork! That's what I like to hear," she said. She pointed to Charge's frill. "See this discoloration here?"

Josh squinted in the half dark. He could just make out a greenish-blue tinge to the skin across the frill. "Yeah. What is it?"

"My guess is infection," said Melissa. "The cut itself is healing, but I reckon infection got in and is spreading through the whole frill."

Josh chewed his lip. "What does that mean? Is Charge going to be OK?" he asked.

Melissa smiled. "He's going to be just fine,

as long as he gets plenty of rest. I've given him a tonic that'll knock that infection right out of him, but he'll have to stay on the ranch for a few days," she said. "No gallivanting off on adventures, no trotting into town. Charge stays right here in his pen until I say otherwise. Got it?"

Much as Josh hated the idea of being without his trusty steed, there was no way he was going to risk Charge getting even sicker. Charge would have come in mighty useful when it came to catching the Blood Claw Bandit, but Josh would just have to manage without him. He gave his dino a pat and nodded at the vet. "Yes, ma'am," he said. "I got it. Charge won't be going anywhere."

That evening, Josh stumbled down the alley beside the town clerk's, stretched, yawned, then squeezed through the gap in the fence. Sam and Abi were both waiting for him.

Sam frowned when he saw their friend. "Wow, you look terrible!" he said.

"Thanks a lot," said Josh.

"He's right," said Abi. "You look like you died and no one told you."

"I've been awake since four thirty this morning," Josh said, yawning again. He gave himself a shake. "I'll be fine. Did you spread the message?"

Josh had sent word to his friends to start a rumor that Sam's dad was getting a late-night delivery of gold bullion for the clerk's office. His whole plan hinged on the Blood Claw Bandit finding out about the gold and making a move—the villain would never be able to resist a big haul of gold. Then, when everything was ready, Josh would spring his trap and claim the five-hundred-dollar reward.

"We told Molly the newsgirl, so everyone from here to the Roaring Jaws Valley will have heard the story by now," said Sam.

Josh grinned, excitement pushing his tiredness away. "Awesome! Did you bring the net?"

Abi held up a net made of tied-together lengths of rope. "Got it."

"The courier should be here any minute," said Sam, glancing at his pocket watch.

Josh and Abi exchanged a glance. "What? The courier is actually coming?" asked Josh. "He's not really bringing gold bullion, is he?"

Sam snorted with laughter. "No! Of course not," he said. "He's bringing walnuts."

"Walnuts?" asked Josh and Abi at exactly the same time.

"Yes," said Sam. "My dad and granddad love them. They get a delivery shipped in every week. But the Blood Claw Bandit doesn't know that. He'll think it's gold bullion!"

Abi clapped Sam on the shoulder. "Wow. And I thought you were the weird one in your family."

There was a scuffing sound from the other side of the fence. Josh and the others scrambled to hide behind a stack of empty wooden boxes in one corner of the yard. They ducked down just as the back gate was opened and a man in a courier's uniform staggered in. The man carried an enormous wooden crate, which, from the way he was walking, seemed to be very heavy. He puffed and panted as he heaved the crate to the middle of the yard, then groaned with the effort as he lowered it to the ground.

"Wow," Josh whispered. "That must be a lot of walnuts."

"And your dad gets one of these delivered *every week*?" asked Abi. "What is he, a squirrel?"

The courier straightened, rubbed his lower back, then hobbled back out of the yard, closing the gate behind him. The three friends looked at each other.

"Now the waiting begins," said Josh.

The waiting began.

And continued.

Aaaaand continued.

"I don't think he's coming," said Abi at last. "Maybe the Blood Claw Bandit didn't get the message."

Night had fully fallen now, and they could barely make out the crate in the faint glow of the half-moon.

"He'll come," said Josh. "He has to."

Just as he spoke, they heard a creak from beyond the fence. Josh and the others held their breath as they heard the latch of the gate slide open. The old hinges creaked as the gate swung inward—it could only be the Blood Claw Bandit.

 76

As one, the three friends raised their heads enough to see over the boxes. A dark figure was tiptoeing into the garden, a long metal bar held in one hand. As they watched, the man slipped the end of the bar under the lid of the crate and began trying to pry it open.

"Ready?" Josh whispered.

Abi nodded.

Sam gulped.

"One…two…"

Josh and Abi jumped up at the same time. "Three!" Josh cried. Sam jumped up behind them.

"I wasn't ready!" he protested, but the others were already swinging into action. They tossed the net over the thief, knocking him to the ground and tangling him in the ropes.

"Got you!" Josh cheered. He and Abi high-fived with excitement. "We caught him! We caught the Blood Claw Bandit!"

"What in tarnation?" spluttered a voice from inside the net.

Sam pushed past his friends and peered down at the wriggling figure on the ground.

"Grandpa?" he asked.

"Huh?" Josh said. He leaned in closer and saw that the person they'd trapped was a wrinkled old man with thinning grey hair.

"I only wanted a few walnuts," Sam's grandfather said. "I didn't see no harm in it. You know how I love my walnuts, Sam."

Sam nodded to the others. "He does love his walnuts."

Abi glanced over at the enormous crate filled with the nuts. "Really? I'd never have guessed."

Josh sighed. "If the bandit was around, we'll have scared him well off by now," he said.

"So it's over then?" asked Sam. "You're giving up?"

Josh shook his head. "Never. We're going to

catch the Blood Claw Bandit, get that reward, and save the ranch," he said. He smiled weakly. "I just have to figure out how…"

CHAPTER 7

Josh sat on the back of Sam's gallimimus, yawning with almost every step the dinosaur took. The ranch was just a half mile up ahead now. The dino's lumbering movements were rocking him to sleep, and he had to give himself a shake to try to stay awake.

"Ugh. Somebody slap me," he said as he yawned.

Smack! Abi leaned over in her saddle and slapped Josh across the cheek.

His eyes went wide. "Ow!" he yelled. "I didn't actually want you to slap me!"

Abi smirked. "Oh. Sorry," she said. "Still, you look much more awake now. Which is more than I can say for some people."

Sam was doubled over, his forehead resting on his dinosaur's neck. He snored softly, then spluttered awake when Josh jabbed him in the ribs.

"Wha—? I'm awake, Mom!" he yelled.

Josh and Abi burst into fits of laughter.

Josh's face fell though when he saw a familiar spindly figure standing in the road ahead. The man was staring at the ranch, occasionally lowering his head to scribble in a notebook.

"What do you want, Malachi?" demanded Josh as they drew level with Amos's uncle.

Malachi reacted in surprise when he saw them.

"Bit early for you three to be roaming around, isn't it?" he asked. His eyes narrowed. "What have you been up to?"

"Nothing!" blurted Sam.

"None of your business," said Josh.

Malachi's face crumpled into a scowl. "Speaking of *business*, let your father know I'll be bringing the deeds along presently." His mouth twisted into a nasty grin. "That ranch of yours will be mine by noon."

"Let's go, Sam," said Josh. "I think I'm gonna barf."

 84

"See you soon, young man," Malachi said and laughed, but Josh didn't look back. He hung on to Sam's saddle and gritted his teeth. Noon was only six hours away. How was he going to save the ranch by then?

A few minutes later, they arrived at the ranch. Josh sensed right away that something was wrong. There were lights on inside the house, meaning Mom and Dad were awake. He'd be in big trouble for sneaking out, but that wasn't what was bothering him.

The gate to Charge's pen creaked gently as it swung back and forth on the breeze. "That shouldn't be open," Josh muttered.

He swung down from Sam's dino and started walking toward the pen. He peered through the narrow gaps in the high fence, searching for any sign of movement inside, but saw none.

Josh broke into a run, his heart thumping in his chest like a drum. "Charge?" he called. "Charge, where are you?"

He skidded through the gate and into the pen.

The *empty* pen.

Josh spun back toward the gate.

"He's gone!" he called to Sam and Abi.

"What?" Abi shouted. "That's impossible!"

If Charge had escaped, then he couldn't have gotten far—Josh hoped. "He's probably over by the house," he told Abi and Sam. "Yeah, that's all. Nothing to worry about…"

Suddenly though, the rest of the sentence stuck in his throat as he spotted something on the ground. His hands shook as he bent down to pick the thing up. It was a claw. A blood-soaked claw.

Josh exploded out of the pen and smacked straight into the side of Abi's dinosaur with a thud. "He took Charge!" Josh gasped. "The Blood Claw Bandit took Charge!"

"Oh no!" Sam said. "We should tell the sheriff."

"The sheriff is useless. You saw what happened when the Blood Claw Bandit robbed the bank. We need to catch him ourselves," said Josh.

"We didn't exactly have a lot of luck with that the last time," Abi reminded him. "What makes you think we'll get him this time?"

Josh clenched his fist around the claw. "Because this time, it's personal!"

Abi nodded solemnly. "So where do we start?"

"Well," Sam began. "It's not like the Blood Claw Bandit can wander around Trihorn on Charge without people noticing him."

Abi agreed. "I reckon he can go unnoticed just about long enough to sell him though."

The others frowned. "It's dino market day," she reminded them. "The auction will be starting in twenty minutes or so."

Josh swung up behind Sam again. "How quickly can this thing get us into town?"

"Uh…thirty minutes, maybe?" Sam said.

Josh felt his stomach flip. "Then hurry," he urged. "We have to get to the market before it's too late!"

Twenty-seven minutes later, Sam's and Abi's dinosaurs skidded to a stop right outside the market. They'd heard the roaring and grunting and growling of the dinos from a whole mile away, and now that they were closer, they could barely hear themselves think.

The market took place once a month in the old rock quarry just west of the town. Sellers would come from all over the county and beyond to trade their wares, with buyers lining up to bid for whichever dinos took their fancy. There were *hundreds* of dinosaurs, packed into pens all around the quarry, and dozens of eager buyers already gathered around the pens.

Josh searched frantically for any sign of Charge. "Can you see him?" he asked. "Sam? Abi?"

Abi pointed sharply off to the left. "Triceratops pen's over there," she called.

"Then that's where he'll be," said Josh, leaping from the saddle and breaking into a sprint.

The pen was surrounded by eager buyers, all shouting and haggling and trying to snap up a bargain before the beasts could go to the auction. Josh ducked his head and elbowed through the crowd, fighting his way to the front. He kept pushing until he reached the fence surrounding the pen. His heart leaped when he spotted Charge standing in the center of the circle, gazing sadly around at the other, much larger triceratops.

"Charge!" Josh yelled, and the dino's big head immediately snapped up. Charge's tongue unrolled, and he galloped across to Josh. The

91

buyers around Josh all jumped back in fright, fearing the dinosaur was about to charge them with his huge horns.

Instead, Charge stopped at the fence and licked the hand that Josh squeezed through.

Charge looked different, but Josh would still have recognized him anywhere. The greenish-blue discoloration on his frill was worse than ever. Josh brushed his fingers across it, then gasped as the color flaked away.

"Paint," he mumbled, but then a hulking figure brushed him aside and rang a handbell with a *clang, clang, clang.*

The auctioneer lowered his bell, and the crowd fell silent. "Our next lot is this very fine young triceratops," he announced, and Josh felt his blood run cold. "Who'll start the bidding? Let's get this dinosaur sold!"

Dinos for Sale

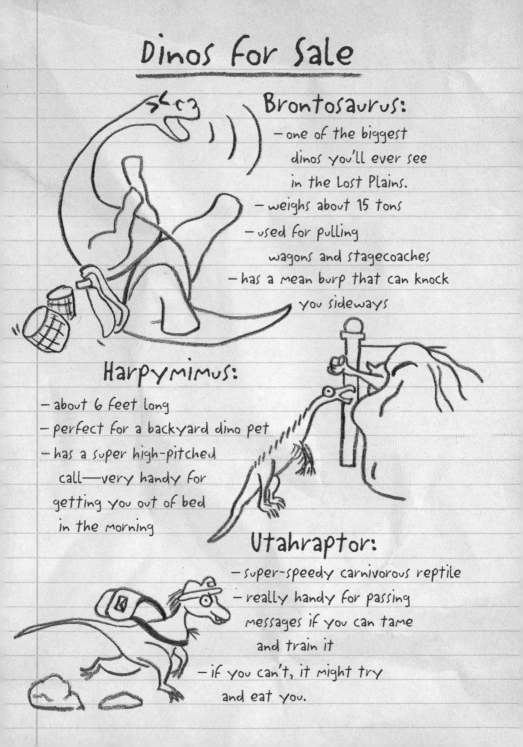

Brontosaurus:
- one of the biggest dinos you'll ever see in the Lost Plains.
- weighs about 15 tons
- used for pulling wagons and stagecoaches
- has a mean burp that can knock you sideways

Harpymimus:
- about 6 feet long
- perfect for a backyard dino pet
- has a super high-pitched call—very handy for getting you out of bed in the morning

Utahraptor:
- super-speedy carnivorous reptile
- really handy for passing messages if you can tame and train it
- if you can't, it might try and eat you.

CHAPTER

8

A few hands shot up in the crowd, and the auctioneer began rattling off numbers. "Ten. Twenty. Thirty on the right. Forty. Do we have fifty?"

"Wait!" Josh yelled, jumping in front of the auctioneer and waving his arms.

The auctioneer pointed at him. "Fifty dollars, thank you, young man!"

"No, I'm not bidding!" Josh said.

The auctioneer frowned. "So you don't want him?"

"I do want him," Josh cried. "Because he's mine! Someone stole him this morning. They've tried to disguise him with paint on his frill. Look." Josh held up his fingers, showing off the flakes of paint.

There was an "ooh" from the crowd.

The auctioneer put his hands on his hips. "Well now, this is highly irregular," he said. He cast his gaze across the faces of the people around him. "Will the seller of this triceratops come forward so we can sort this mess out?"

Everyone in the crowd began glancing suspiciously at everyone else. For the first time ever, complete silence fell over the market.

"There!" yelled Abi, breaking the hush. A dark-clad figure on a velociraptor shot out from behind one of the pens and began racing for the horizon.

"The Blood Claw Bandit!" cried Josh. "Charge, come on, buddy. We have to catch him!"

"What? You can't just take this dinosaur!" the auctioneer cried.

"Sorry, but I wasn't asking." He stepped aside just as Charge exploded through the fence, shattering the wood into splinters. With a "Yah," Josh swung up into the saddle, and the world became a blur as Charge set off in pursuit of the fleeing bandit.

The velociraptor was fast, but Charge was faster. He started to gain ground almost immediately. "You won't get away, bandit!" Josh shouted.

The bandit turned in his saddle, surprised by the voice so close behind him. The wind caught his hat and tore it off. Josh's eyes went wide when he spotted the shock of bright-red hair tied up on the bandit's head.

"Melissa Barnstable!" Josh gasped. He realized the bandit had been right there in front of him all along, and he'd let him...*her*...get away.

The vet turned and shot a malicious glance his way. "Get out of here, young'un. Or you're gonna end up on the wrong side of this here pistol."

Josh saw Melissa reach for her gleaming silver gun. It looked mighty fierce, but the Blood Claw Bandit hadn't reckoned on the power of a raging triceratops and a trusty lasso.

"We'll see about that," he cried.

Josh reached for his rope and began twirling it above his head as Charge closed in on the velociraptor. Carefully, he took aim.

With a flick of Josh's wrist, the rope sailed through the air.

"Bull's-eye!" Josh cheered as the loop dropped over the bandit, the gun falling out of her hand. Josh wrapped the rope around Charge's horns, and the triceratops skidded to a halt. The rope tightened, and Melissa gave a yelp as she was jerked backward out of her saddle.

The velociraptor turned, jaws snapping, only to find three long horns lowered and ready to charge. The raptor glanced down at its rider on the ground, then back at the deadly looking horns. It began to back away, slowly at first, then quickly breaking into a run. In seconds, it was halfway to the horizon, leaving Melissa to fend for herself.

"You're no vet," Josh said. "You're a charlatan and a thief."

Melissa smiled. "What? No! You've got the wrong gal. That thing with the gun... It was just a little misunderstanding!" she said.

Josh pointed to the ground beside her. A leather pouch had fallen from her belt, scattering a dozen bloodied claws on the sand.

Melissa's face went pale. "Oh, those? Uh, those are...those are..." She sighed. "I got nothing."

There was a commotion from behind Josh as Sam, Abi, and the sheriff arrived on the scene. The sheriff swung down from his saddle and slapped a pair of handcuffs over Melissa's wrists.

"Mighty fine work there, Josh," the sheriff

said, tipping his hat. "And to think she was posing as a dino vet…"

Melissa shot Josh a mean look. "You won't keep the Blood Claw Bandit down for long," she cackled. "You mark my words!"

"Yeah, yeah," Abi said. "Save it for the judge."

The sheriff hauled Barnstable over his dino and tied her up for good measure.

"Thanks," said Josh. "But, erm, I was just wondering…"

"Yes?" asked the sheriff.

"The reward!" Abi and Sam burst out.

"You've earned every penny," he said. "I'll drop it around to your place once I've got this here bandit safely under lock and key."

Josh, Sam, and Abi all cheered. "We did it!" Josh cried.

"You saved the ranch!" Abi said and laughed.

Josh swung back up into Charge's saddle. "Thanks for all your help, guys. I gotta go tell my mom and dad the good news!" Josh tipped his hat to Melissa. She scowled up at him and stuck out her tongue, and Josh laughed as he turned Charge around and raced all the way home.

"Mom, Dad, you'll never believe it!" he hollered as he burst into the kitchen. He stopped when he saw his dad sitting at the table with a pen in his hand, scribbling his name at the bottom of a contract. Malachi Wilks leaned over him, rubbing his hands with glee.

"Wait, stop!" Josh cried. "What are you doing here? You said you were coming at noon!"

Malachi grinned. "I was so excited about owning this place, I couldn't wait a moment longer," he said. He gave Josh's dad a pat on the shoulder. "Now, finish signing, there's a good chap."

Dad's jaw clenched, and his hand tightened on the pen. He met Josh's eye. "Sorry, son. We have to!"

"No, we don't!" Josh said. He blurted out the whole story and watched his mom's and dad's eyes getting wider and wider.

"And the sheriff's going to bring the money today!" he finished. "All five hundred dollars."

Dad looked down at the contract. He quietly

set the pen down on the table, then picked up the thick pile of paper. With one swift movement, he tore the whole thing in half. "I'm sorry, Mr. Wilks. The ranch is not for sale."

"What?" screeched Malachi. "You can't do this! We had a deal! I own this place!"

Dad stood up. He towered above the much smaller Malachi, who took one look at Dad's broad chest and immediately stopped talking.

"No. My family owns this place," Dad said. He smiled at Josh. "And that's how it's going to stay."

Mom took Josh's hand, and they both stood at Dad's side. "Now get out of our family's home, Mr. Wilks," Mom said. "And I'd appreciate it if you didn't come back."

Malachi glared at them all. He opened his

mouth to say something, but the look on Mom's face told him it probably wasn't a good idea. "Fine," he muttered, stomping toward the door. "See if I care!"

The moment the front door slammed closed, Mom and Dad both turned and wrapped their arms around Josh. They'd have enough money to rebuild the barn ahead of winter, and they didn't have to work for weaselly old Malachi Wilks.

"I'd say this deserves a celebratory pie," Mom said with a laugh.

"Forget pie," Dad said. "We're throwing a party!"

Josh smiled. He'd caught the bandit, rescued Charge, and saved the ranch. Not bad for a day's work, he reckoned!

Don't miss the rest of Josh's adventures!

How to Tame a Triceratops

Book 1

Josh Sanders wants to be the next great dinosaur cowboy—ropin' raptors and ridin' bucking brontosauruses just like his hero, Terrordactyl Bill!

Too bad he's stuck working on his family's iguanodon ranch. The closest Josh has ever been to a T. rex is reading about them in his Dino Rider Handbook.

But Josh is ready to prove he has what it takes to win the annual settlement race. And with the help of his friends, Josh is going to tame the fastest triceratops he can find.

How to Rope a Giganotosaurus

Book 2

Josh Sanders will do whatever it takes to become the next great dinosaur cowboy!

So when news breaks that legendary dino wrangler Terrordactyl Bill has captured a T. rex, it's clear to Josh that it's time to follow in the footsteps of his personal hero. But how the heck is he supposed to top nabbing a T. rex?

Josh knows what he needs to do: bag himself a giganotosaurus, the biggest, baddest meat eater in existence! It's gonna take a whole lotta rope to pull this one off…

How to Hog-Tie a T-Rex

Book 3

It's time for the families of Trihorn to participate in the annual iguanadon drive to Scaly Point—a treacherous journey of some five hundred miles. Josh Sanders and his friends Abi and Sam are thrilled to join the drive...

until an avalanche comes down and cuts them off from the group!

To top it off, Josh's archnemesis, Amos, is trapped with them. With no other choice, the gang will have to band together to make it back to Scaly Point—and escape a bloodthirsty T-Rex!

ABOUT THE AUTHOR

Ever since he was a little boy, Will Dare has been mad about T. rexes and velociraptors. He always wondered what it would be like to live in a world where they were still alive. Now, grown up, he has put pen to paper and imagined just that world. Will lives in rural America with his wife and his best pal, Charge (a dog, not a triceratops).